Based on Walt Disney's
full-length animated movie

Adapted by Jan Carr

SCHOLASTIC INC.
New York Toronto London Auckland Sydney

ISBN 0-590-41913-7

 Adapted from the Walt Disney motion picture PETER PAN, based upon PETER PAN by Sir James Matthew Barrie, by arrangements with the Hospital for Sick Children, London, England. Published by Scholastic Inc.

12 11 10 9 8 7 6 5 4 3 2 9/8 0 1 2 3 4/9

Printed in the U.S.A.
First Scholastic printing, July 1989

Peter Pan

1

All over the world, there are families with children. Some children are round and some are thin as sticks. Some children are sassy and some polite. But this much is sure — as each day passes, children get older and start to grow up.

It was happening in the Darling house, though Peter Pan didn't know it. The Darlings had three children, Wendy, John, and Michael. All three of the children believed in Peter Pan. Every night, Wendy, the oldest, told her two brothers stories about Peter and the Lost Boys. Peter Pan himself loved the stories. Sometimes he came to listen outside the window of the Darlings' cozy London home.

On this particular night, the children were playing in the nursery. John and Michael were dueling with toy swords. Michael was pretending he was Peter Pan and John was playing Captain Hook.

"Take that!" shouted Michael. He jabbed his brother with his sword. "Give up, Captain Hook?"

"Blast you, Peter Pan!" cried John. He had made a hook out of a coat hanger. Wendy walked by and noticed something wrong.

"No, John," she said. "It was the left hand."

John changed the hanger from his right hand to the left.

"Thank you, Wendy," he said, and got right back to dueling.

The three children had a nursemaid, Nana, who was a rather unusual nursemaid. She was a dog. They also had a mother, Mrs. Darling, and a father, Mr. Darling.

That night, while the children were playing, Mr. and Mrs. Darling were getting ready to go to a party. Mrs. Darling was primping in front of the mirror. Mr. Darling was rummaging through his dresser drawers.

"Mary," he said, "unless I find my cuff links we can't go to the party."

Mr. Darling searched all through his bedroom, but his cuff links were gone. He wandered into the nursery.

"Have you seen my cuff links?" he asked the boys.

"Cuff links, Father?" asked John. "Michael, the buried treasure — where is it?"

Michael shrugged his shoulders. "I don't know," he said.

"The map, then," said John. "Where is the treasure map?"

"It got lost," said Michael.

Mr. Darling searched through the mess on the nursery floor. He pushed back the covers on John's bed.

"Good heavens!" he cried. "My shirt front! What's it doing in the nursery?"

Mr. Darling picked up the starched white shirt front and started to button it across his chest.

"Hooray!" Michael called. "You found it! You found the treasure map!"

On the front of the shirt there was, indeed, a treasure map. The boys had drawn it there.

"No!" cried Mr. Darling, when he saw what they had done. "NO-O-O-O-O!"

2

Mrs. Darling bustled into the nursery. She was dressed in high style, ready for the party, but waiting for her husband. Mr. Darling held the shirt front out for her to see.

"Mary, look!" he said.

"It's only chalk, Father," said Michael.

"Michael!" Mrs. Darling started to scold.

"It's not his fault," said John. "It's in the story. And Wendy said . . ."

"Wendy?" Mr. Darling boomed. He should have known that Wendy was at the bottom of this. Those silly stories she told were disrupting the entire household. He'd have to set his daughter straight. He called her into the room.

"Yes, Father?" said Wendy. She saw the mottled shirt front. "Why, Father," she said. "What have you done to your shirt?"

"Me?" shouted Mr. Darling. "What have *I* done?" He groaned in despair. This was not at all the way he expected a family to run. A family was supposed to be organized. A family was supposed to run smoothly.

"Now, George, really," Mrs. Darling said calmly. "It comes right off."

Mrs. Darling wet a handkerchief and wiped it across the shirt. The chalk came off easily. She wiped the shirt front clean.

"That's no excuse!" shouted Mr. Darling. He turned to face his daughter. "Haven't I warned you?" he said to her sternly. "Stuffing the boys with a lot of silly stories!"

"Oh, but they aren't silly," Wendy protested.

"I say they are!" shouted Mr. Darling. "Captain Crook! Peter Pirate!"

"Peter Pan, Father," Wendy corrected him.

"Pan! Pirate! Poppycock!" yelled Mr. Darling. "Absolute poppycock! And let me tell you, this ridiculous — "

"Now, George," Mrs. Darling cut in. She tried to soothe her husband's temper. She smoothed back his hair and straightened his tie. But Mr. Darling would not be calmed.

"Mary," he said. His voice grew stern. He glanced at his daughter. He made a quick decision. "The child's growing up," he said. "It's high time she had a room of her own."

Across the room, Nana gasped.

"Father!" cried Wendy.

"George!" cried Mrs. Darling.

"No!" cried Michael.

All the family was in shock. He couldn't mean it! Take Wendy from the nursery?

"I mean it!" Mr. Darling repeated. "Young lady, this is your last night in the nursery."

Wendy hung her head.

"And that's my last word on the matter," Mr. Darling snapped.

The children's father had stated his piece. He turned to stride out of the room.

3

Mr. Darling never got past the doorway of the nursery. Nana was lying in his path, but he didn't see the big, woolly dog. He tripped and stumbled over her. Nana yelped. Mr. Darling slipped and landed on a small toy wagon.

"Oh!" he cried. The wagon took off and skidded across the floor.

The family ran to help their faithful dog.

"Poor Nana!" they cried.

Mr. Darling got up and brushed himself off.

"Poor Nana!" he said angrily. His family worried more about the dog than they worried about him! "This is the last straw!" He grabbed Nana by the collar and dragged her out of the room. "Out, I say!"

Little Michael ran after his nursemaid.

"No, Father! No!" he cried.

Mr. Darling dragged Nana down the stairs. "There'll be no more dogs for nursemaids in this house!" he proclaimed.

Mr. Darling pulled the dog out to the yard, tied a rope around her collar, and tethered her to a tree. Nana looked up at him with her big, sad, brown eyes. Mr. Darling softened.

"Dash it all, Nana," he said. "Don't look at me like that. It's just that you're not really a nurse at all. You're a dog. And the children aren't puppies. They're people. And sooner or later, Nana, people have to grow up."

Upstairs in the nursery, Mrs. Darling hustled the children into their beds and tucked them into their clean, fresh sheets. She planted a good-night kiss on each of their foreheads.

"The buried treasure," Michael said. He held something tightly in his warm, moist hand. Mr. Darling's cuff links had been found at last.

Mrs. Darling smiled and took the cuff links. She walked over to the nursery window to lock it against the night.

"Oh, don't lock it, Mother," said Wendy. "He might come back."

"He?" Mrs. Darling asked, puzzled.

"Yes," said Wendy. "Peter Pan. You see, I found something that belongs to him. His shadow. Nana had it, but I took it away."

"Yes, of course, dear," Mrs. Darling said. "Good night." She turned off the nursery light and went to join her husband.

"George," she asked him, "do you think the

children will be safe without Nana?"

"Of course they'll be safe," said Mr. Darling.

Mrs. Darling wasn't so sure. "Wendy said something about a shadow," she said. "She said it was Peter Pan's."

"Peter Pan's!" Mr. Darling laughed. "Goodness gracious! Sound the alarm! Call Scotland Yard!"

Mr. Darling did not believe in Peter Pan.

"Oh, Mary," he chided his wife. "Peter Pan, indeed! You're as bad as the children. No wonder Wendy gets those idiotic ideas!"

Mr. and Mrs. Darling stepped out of the house and locked the door behind them. The children were alone in the nursery. Nana was locked outside.

4

In the quiet nursery, the children slept soundly. Outside, a nimble figure flew down from the sky and perched on their windowsill. With him was a tiny, glittering fairy sprite. The boy was Peter Pan. The fairy was Tinker Bell. They peered into the children's window and slipped inside.

"Over here, Tink!" Peter whispered. "Must be here somewhere."

Peter looked around the room. He was looking for his shadow. Tinker Bell flew above him while Peter searched the room.

"Shadow! Oh, Shadow!" he called.

Tink landed on the edge of the dresser. The top drawer had a keyhole. Tink peered in and squinted into the darkness.

"It's in here," she jingled. Tinker Bell's voice was like a thousand tinkling bells.

Peter slid the drawer open. When Tink flew inside, the shadow darted out.

"Hey!" Peter cried. He slammed the drawer shut. The shadow had escaped, but Tinker Bell was trapped inside.

Peter leaped up at the shadow. The shadow skittered up the wall. Peter chased it across the ceiling. The shadow zipped down and hid behind a chair.

"Aha!" Peter cried. He lunged at his shadow, slid under Wendy's bed, and crashed against the soapstand. He had caught his shadow and held it firmly by its foot.

Wendy sat up in bed and blinked.

"Peter Pan!" she cried. "Oh, Peter, I knew you'd come back!"

Inside the dresser drawer, Tink jingled and sparked. She tried to squeeze out of the keyhole, but it was too small.

"You know, Peter," Wendy said, "you look exactly the way I thought you would."

Peter sat down on the floor and picked up a bar of soap. He rubbed it on the foot of his shadow then pressed his own foot against it hard.

"Peter!" Wendy laughed. "You can't stick a shadow on with soap. It needs sewing. That's the proper way."

Wendy got out her sewing basket and took the shadow from Peter. She threaded a silvery needle with strong black cord and began to stitch the shadow back onto Peter, where it belonged. Peter watched her.

"My name is Wendy," Wendy introduced herself.

Peter took out his pan pipes and played a little tune.

"How did Nana get your shadow?" Wendy asked.

"Jumped at me the other night," Peter said. "At the window."

"What were you doing at the window?" Wendy asked.

"I came to listen to the stories," said Peter.

"My stories?" Wendy asked. She was surprised. "But they're all about you."

" 'Course," Peter grinned. "That's why I like 'em. I tell 'em to the Lost Boys."

Wendy put the finishing stitches on the shadow.

"Oh," she sighed. "I'm so glad you came back tonight. I might never have seen you." Her voice grew grave. "You know," she said, "I have to grow up tomorrow. Tonight's my last night in the nursery."

"Grow up!" Peter jumped up, startled. "But that means no more stories!"

Peter grabbed Wendy's hand.

"No!" he cried. "I won't have it! Come on!"

"But where are we going?" asked Wendy.

"To Never Land!" Peter crowed.

"Never Land!" Wendy cried happily.

Inside the drawer Tinker Bell knocked against the keyhole and jingled wildly.

5

Wendy's skin tingled at the thought of going to Never Land.

"You'll never grow up there," Peter promised.

If she were really going to go, she had a lot of things to do. Wendy ran about the nursery. She had to pack her bags. She had to leave a note.

"Oh, Peter," she cried. "I'm so happy. I think I'll give you a kiss!"

Inside the dresser, Tinker Bell picked up a pair of scissors and pried open the drawer. Peter Pan was *her* boyfriend. She wasn't about to let Wendy kiss him. Tinker Bell was jealous!

As Wendy puckered her lips to kiss Peter, someone grabbed her hair and yanked her back. Hard.

"Ow!" cried Wendy.

"Stop it, Tink!" said Peter. He snatched off his cap and chased Tink around the nursery.

Michael and John woke up and rubbed their eyes.

"He's here!" shouted Michael.

"Jiminee!" shouted John.

Peter caught up to Tinker Bell and clapped his hat over the little pixie.

"Tinker Bell," he said, presenting her to Wendy. "Don't know what's got into her."

Tinker Bell jingled angrily. Peter Pan just laughed. He clapped his hat back on his head and hopped up on the windowsill.

"Come on, Wendy. Let's go," he said.

"We're going to Never Land," Wendy told John and Michael excitedly. "Peter's taking us. But, Peter," Wendy asked suddenly, "how do we get to Never Land?"

"Fly, of course," said Peter.

"Fly!" Wendy's eyes opened wide.

"It's easy," said Peter. "All you have to do is think a lovely thought."

Wendy closed her eyes to think. So did Michael and John.

"Like toys at Christmas?" said Wendy.

"Sleighbells? Snow?" said John.

As the children thought of lovely thoughts, they began to rise. They floated up in the air. Peter took their hands. They flew higher. But when Peter let go, the children dropped through the air and fell on the bed.

"Oh," Peter laughed. "Something I forgot. Pixie dust!"

He grabbed hold of Tinker Bell and gave her a gentle shake. Bright, sparkling dust fell off of Tink and onto the children.

"Think the happiest things," Peter instructed again.

The children floated right up in the air.

"We can fly!" they cried.

"Come on, everybody!" said Peter.

Peter flew out the window, and the others followed. In the yard below, Nana saw the children flying away from the nursery. She pulled frantically at her rope. The children flew after Peter and disappeared into the glittering night sky.

6

Never Land is a magical place, but it has its share of trouble. Peter, Wendy, and the boys didn't know it, but they were flying into danger. Captain Hook was waiting for them. Captain Hook and his pirates.

The pirates were sitting on their ship in the harbor of the island. They were restless. They were bored. They wanted to push out to sea, to steal and kill. They sharpened their knives and practiced their aim.

Captain Hook sat on deck, looking over his map.

"Blast that Peter Pan!" he cried. "If only I could find his hideout, I'd trap him in his lair. But where is it?"

The captain ran his steely hook across the map.

"Mermaid Lagoon?" he said. "No. We've searched that. We've combed Cannibal Cove. And Pan can't be in Indian Territory. Hmm," he stopped. "The Indians." That gave him an idea.

"The Indians know this island better than I do my own ship."

Mr. Smee, the first mate, walked up to give the captain his morning shave. The captain grabbed Smee by the collar.

"I've got it!" Hook cried. "Tiger Lily, Smee! Tiger Lily, the chief's daughter! She'll know where Pan is hiding!"

The captain laughed a cold, sharp laugh.

"I'll get back at Pan!" he said. "I'll get back at Pan for *this!*" He waved his hooked hand through the air and thrust its sharp point in Smee's face.

"Why, Cap'n," Smee gulped, "when Peter Pan cut your hand off it was only a childish prank, you might say."

"Aye," said Hook, "but throwing it to that crocodile was worse. That cursed beast liked the taste of me so much, he's followed me ever since, licking his chops for the rest of me."

"Aye, Cap'n," said Smee. "And the crocodile would've had you for sure by now if he hadn't swallowed that alarm clock."

It was true. The crocodile that was chasing after Hook had an alarm clock in his belly. "Tic-toc! Tic-toc!" it went. Loudly. Whenever the crocodile came near, Captain Hook could hear him, and it gave him time to escape.

Mr. Smee lathered up Hook's chin for the shave.

"Tic-toc," came a sound. "Tic-toc." Captain Hook jumped into Smee's arms.

"Save me, Smee!" he cried. "Save me!"

Smee looked over the railing of the ship. There, in the water below, was the crocodile. He was swimming in circles. His eyes were mean and hungry.

"Here now!" Smee yelled down. "Shame on you! There'll be no handouts today. Go on! Shoo! Shoo!"

The crocodile slipped back down under the water.

"All clear, Cap'n," said Smee. "Nothin' to worry about."

The captain lay back in his chair. Above them, in the crow's nest, one of the pirates spotted something, something flying in sight of the ship.

"Peter Pan ahoy!" he shouted. "Three points off starboard bow!"

Hook jumped up and grabbed his telescope. Sure enough, there was Pan, flying over Never Land. He had a girl with him, and two young boys.

"All hands on deck!" shouted Smee. "All hands on deck!"

At his call, scores of pirates came tumbling up through the hatch. They ran to load the cannon. They aimed it at Peter and lit the fuse.

7

As Peter led Wendy and the boys over Never Land, they looked down at the beautiful island.

"Oh, Peter," said Wendy. "It's just as I've always dreamed it would be. Look, there's Mermaid Lagoon."

"And the Indian encampment," said John.

"And look!" shouted Michael. "There's Cap'n Hook and the pirates!"

As Michael spotted the pirates, the pirates took aim.

BOOM! A cannonball hurtled through the sky.

"Look out!" cried Peter. He pushed his friends behind a cloud. The cannonball hurtled by.

"Quick, Tink!" Peter shouted. "Take Wendy and the boys to the island. I'll stay here and draw Hook's fire."

Another cannonball whizzed at them. Peter leaped out of its path. Wendy, John, and Michael flew quickly after Tink.

"Tinker Bell!" shouted Wendy. "Wait for us!"

Tinker Bell was light and fleet. She knew where she was going and sped through the air. She heard Wendy calling, but she didn't care. She had plans for Wendy, and they weren't very pretty.

Tink dove down toward the island and through the trees. On the trunk of one tree was an odd, gnarled knothole. Tink flew right through. Inside, the tree trunk was hollow. It led to a secret passageway and down to an underground grotto. The Lost Boys slept in the grotto. One was dressed as a bear cub, another as a young fox. They were all Peter's friends.

Tinker Bell buzzed at the boys to wake them. She grabbed a club and shoved it into the little bear cub's arms. She jingled a message.

"Huh?" the boys said. "Orders from Pan?"

Tink jingled more. "A terrible Wendy Bird!" she said. "Flying this way!"

The boys jumped up from their beds.

"What're the orders, Tink?" they cried.

"Shoot it down!" Tink lied. "Peter says to shoot it down!"

The boys grabbed their slingshots and raced up through the tree. They spotted the Wendy Bird, flying above them. If Peter Pan said to shoot it, that's what they would do.

"Ready! Aim! FIRE!" they cried.

8

The shots grazed Wendy and she started to fall, but Peter Pan flew beneath her and caught her in his arms. The two floated gently to the ground. The Lost Boys ran up and surrounded Peter.

"We followed your orders, Pan," they said. "We felled the Wendy Bird."

" 'Ten-shun!" Peter cried.

The boys jumped to order.

"I'm certainly proud of you blockheads," Peter shouted angrily. "I bring you a mother to tell you stories and you shoot her down."

"Mother?" said Cubby the bear. "Tink said it was a bird."

"She said to shoot it down," said the rabbit.

"Tinker Bell!" Peter yelled. "Come here!"

Tinker Bell turned her back to Peter. She let out a big, bored yawn.

"You're charged with high treason," Peter said.

"Are you guilty or not guilty? Don't you know you might have killed her?"

Tinker Bell sniffed haughtily.

"I hereby banish you forever!" Peter said.

"Please, not forever!" Wendy intervened.

"Well, for a week then," said Peter. "Come on, Wendy. I'll show you the island."

While Peter and Wendy flew off to tour Never Land, John, Michael, and the Lost Boys tramped off into the woods. Peter had put John in charge of the boys. John decided to take his troop on an adventure, a mission to track down Indians. He led the boys deeper into the forest.

"Halt!" John stopped short. In the center of the path he spied a footprint. "Indians!" he cried. "Blackfoot tribe."

"Let's go get 'em!" said Cubby.

"First," said John, "we must plan our strategy."

The boys huddled in a circle around John to listen to his plan. They didn't notice that the trees around them had started to move. The trees walked forward. They encircled the boys.

Michael was the only boy to look up and notice these most unusual trees. He touched one. He lifted up a branch and peeked. There was a person underneath.

"Indians!" he cried.

The Indians pounced on the boys and captured every last one. They carried the boys off to their camp and tied them to a totem pole. The Indian chief came out of his tepee. He looked angry. He walked gravely over to the boys.

"For many moons," he said, "red man fight pale-face Lost Boys. Sometime you win. Sometime we win."

"Okay, Chief," said Cubby. "You win this time. Now turn us loose."

John looked at Cubby in surprise.

"He's going to turn us loose?" John asked. "You mean this is only a game?"

"Sure," said Foxy. "When we win, we turn them loose and when they win, they turn us loose."

The chief stood firm and shook his head.

"This time no turn 'em loose," he said. He glared at the boys fiercely. "Where you hide Princess Tiger Lily?"

"Tiger Lily?" said Cubby. "We haven't seen her."

"You lie!" cried the chief. "Tiger Lily gone. You took her!"

The chief motioned to one of his braves. The brave took up his drum and began to beat out a war chant.

"If Tiger Lily not back by sunset," the chief threatened, "Lost Boys burn at stake!"

9

High above the Indian camp, Peter and Wendy flew over the island, toward Mermaid Lagoon.

The mermaids who lived there were thrilled to see Peter.

"Hello, Peter!" they called. "We've missed you."

The mermaids swam up to him, chattering noisily. Peter cocked his ear.

"Shhhh!" he said, suddenly. "Quiet!"

He jumped behind a rock and peered down at the water below. In the water was a rowboat. In the rowboat were Captain Hook, Mr. Smee, and Tiger Lily. Tiger Lily's hands were bound together with rope.

"It's Hook!" Peter said. "He's captured Tiger Lily!"

Wendy clambered up to Peter's rock.

"Looks like they're heading for Skull Rock,"

Peter whispered. "Come on. Let's see what they're up to."

Peter grabbed Wendy's hand and the two flew off to follow the boat.

When the boat got to Skull Rock, Smee moored it inside. The sea was rising. The waves lapped up and spilled into the crevices of the hollow rock.

"Now, my dear princess," Hook said to Tiger Lily, "this is my proposition: You tell me the hiding place of Peter Pan and I shall set you free."

Tiger Lily pursed her lips. She would not betray her friend.

"You'd better talk to me, dear," Hook threatened. "For soon the tide will be in, and then it will be too late."

Peter crouched, watching, on a cliff above.

"Stay here, Wendy," he whispered, "and watch the fun."

Peter flew down, close to Hook, and hid in a crevice of the rock.

"Manatoa, Great Spirit of mighty sea water," he called, "speak!" His voice was loud and commanding and echoed over the water. It sounded like an Indian spirit. "Captain Hook!" he called, eerily. "Beware! Beware!"

Hook looked up, startled.

"Did you hear that, Smee?" he said. "Stand by while I take a look around." Hook drew his sword and climbed up the rock to investigate. When he had left the boat, Peter flew closer.

"Mr. Smee!" Peter called. This time he imitated Hook's own voice.

"Captain?" said Mr. Smee.

"Release the princess," Peter instructed. "And take her back to her people."

"But, Cap'n!" said Smee.

"Those are my orders," Peter said sternly.

Mr. Smee set his oars and started to row the princess back to land.

Peter chuckled quietly at his trick, but Mr. Smee didn't get very far. Hook spotted the boat just as it started to glide away. He stuck his foot out from around the edge of the rock and stopped the boat.

"And just what do you think you are doing, Mr. Smee?" he asked.

10

Mr. Smee stared, confused, at the captain's boot.

"I'm doing what you told me, Cap'n," he said. "Carrying out your orders."

"My orders?" Hook boomed.

"Why yes, Cap'n," said Smee. "Didn't you say to set her free?"

"You bumbling, blithering idiot!" Hook shouted. "Put her back!" Hook pushed the boat back.

Peter cleared his throat and again called out to Smee in Hook's voice. "What exactly do you think you're doing?" he asked.

"Putting her back, like you said, Cap'n," Smee said.

"I said nothing of the sort!" Peter shouted. "Take the princess back to her people! Do you understand?"

Smee fell back into the boat. Now he was really confused. Hook, though, had heard Peter's voice.

He climbed around the rock to investigate.

"It's Peter Pan!" he cried.

Hook lunged at Peter with his sword. Peter flew up out of reach.

"Watch this," Peter called to Wendy, who was still on the cliff. Peter dove back down at Hook. He grabbed Hook's pistol from his holster and tossed it to Mr. Smee.

"Try your luck, Mr. Smee?" he laughed.

"Let Pan have it!" Hook yelled to Smee. "Blast him, you idiot!"

Just as Smee was taking aim, Peter ducked behind the captain.

"Right here, Mr. Smee!" Peter called.

Smee pulled the trigger. Hook fell back in the water.

"I'm afraid we've lost the dear captain," Peter said.

But Hook had not been shot, he'd simply lost his balance. He climbed back out of the water and crept up the cliff behind Peter. Hook raised his sword to stab the boy in the back. Peter whirled around and drew his dagger.

"Peter!" shouted Wendy.

"Cleave him to the brisket, Cap'n!" shouted Smee.

Peter and Captain Hook battled at the edge of the cliff. Peter sprang at Hook and knocked him over the edge. Hook skittered down the sheer face of the rock and grabbed a handhold with his hook. He dangled by one arm, just above the water.

"I say, Captain," Peter called down. "Do you hear something?"

From under the water, close to Hook, came a muffled ticking sound. It drew closer and louder. The crocodile! It had followed Hook and was going to eat him!

"No!" Hook shouted.

The crocodile broke the surface of the water and opened his mouth wide. His teeth were sharp and gleaming. He snapped at Hook's coattail and then grabbed at the seat of his pants. Hook fell right into the crocodile's mouth.

"Stay right there, Cap'n!" shouted Smee. "I'll save you!"

Smee hit the crocodile on the snout and knocked him underwater. Hook bounced out of the animal's mouth and scrambled back up through the water toward the rowboat. The crocodile opened his jaws and swam toward the captain. Hook splashed through the water desperately.

"Peter!" shouted Wendy. "What about Tiger Lily?"

Peter jumped down into Skull Rock and scooped the princess up in his arms. He and Tiger Lily flew off to safety, and Wendy flew right behind.

11

Captain Hook escaped the crocodile, at least for the time being. He huddled, wet and shivering, in his cabin, and soaked his feet in a tub of hot water.

"That cursed Peter Pan!" he muttered. "Ahchoo!" he sneezed. "Oh, my head."

Mr. Smee was standing outside the captain's cabin, hammering a "Do Not Disturb" sign onto the door. Another pirate arrived with a fresh kettle of steaming hot water for Hook's tub. Hook opened the door to bring it in. BANG! Smee knocked the captain on the head with his hammer.

"Ahhh!" The captain staggered back into the cabin and fell into a chair. The blow knocked him out cold. He sat dazed, with a silly grin on his face.

"It's nice to see you smiling again," Mr. Smee chuckled. "Like the old days, when we was scuttlin' ships and cuttin' throats. Oh, Captain," he sighed, "why don't we put out to sea again?

There's trouble brewing on this island. Woman trouble. I heard that Pan banished Tinker Bell."

At this news, the captain came to.

"Pan banished Tinker Bell?" he blinked. "But why?"

"Well, on account of Wendy, Cap'n," said Smee. "Tink tried to do her in, she did. Tink's horrible jealous."

The captain scratched his head with his hook.

"That's it, Smee!" he said. "A jealous sweetheart can be tricked into anything. If we convince the pixie we're eager to help her, she might help us find Pan's hiding place."

"But I thought we were going to leave, Cap'n," Smee whined. "Set sail for the Spanish Main."

"No!" Hook shouted. "Smee, you go ashore. Pick up Tinker Bell and bring her to me." Hook picked Smee up by the collar and tossed him out the door. "Understand?" Hook yelled.

Smee stood back up on his feet and dusted himself off.

"Aye-aye, Cap'n," he said.

12

When Peter Pan flew back to the Indian camp with Tiger Lily safe in his arms, the Indian chief let out a grateful cry. He untied all the Lost Boys and gathered his braves around him.

"What's he doing?" asked Wendy. The chief was gesturing to the braves with his hands.

"He's talking in sign language," John explained. "He says, 'Peter Pan mighty warrior. Save Tiger Lily. Make Chief glad.' "

The chief lifted a colorful feather headdress and placed it on Peter Pan's head.

"Make Peter Pan Big Chief," he explained. "You now 'Little Flying Eagle.' "

The chief was inducting Peter into the tribe and making him a chief, too! This was cause for celebration. The Lost Boys all cheered. Tiger Lily got out the peace pipe. The braves began to chant and dance.

When Wendy saw everyone dancing, she jumped up to join them. She started to dance toward Peter, but before she reached him, a squaw tapped her on the shoulder.

"No dance," the squaw said to Wendy. "Get firewood."

Wendy shrugged and followed the squaw to the edge of the camp.

Back in the inner circle, Tiger Lily hopped up on a drum and began dancing for Peter. Peter jumped up on the drum with her, and Tiger Lily rubbed her nose affectionately against his. Just at that moment, Wendy came back with an armload of firewood. She saw Peter rubbing noses with the Indian princess. Now it was her turn to be jealous. Wendy threw down the firewood and stared at Peter.

"No get firewood," she said. "I'm going home!"

She stomped off into the woods and back to the underground hideout.

Wendy was not the only angry girl in the camp. Tinker Bell was there, too. She sat glumly on a branch of a tree, watching the festivities. Mr. Smee crept up behind her. He slipped off his cap and clapped it over the little pixie.

"Beggin' your pardon, Miss Bell," he said. "But Captain Hook would like a word with you."

13

Captain Hook knew that he would have to handle Tinker Bell very carefully. He would have to wheedle and coax the little pixie. He would have to trick her. Above all, he mustn't let her know his real plan. When Mr. Smee brought the tiny fairy in, Captain Hook was sitting at his piano, playing a calm and soothing song.

"Ah, Miss Bell," he said. He sighed sweetly. "Well, Captain Hook admits defeat. Tomorrow I leave the island, never to return. And that's why I asked you over, my dear. To tell Peter that I bear him no ill will."

Tink watched the pirate warily.

"Oh, Pan has his faults, to be sure," Hook continued. "Bringing that Wendy to the island, for instance."

Wendy! Tink tossed her head defiantly at the mention of Wendy's name.

"Rumor has it that she's come between you and Peter," said Hook.

Hangmans Tree
CROCODILE CREEK

Tears welled up in Tinker Bell's eyes. She sniffled and wiped the back of her hand across her cheek.

"Then it's true!" Hook cried.

Tink nodded her head.

"Well, we mustn't judge Peter too harshly," said Hook. "It's that Wendy who's to blame. We've got to save the lad from her clutches. But how? We sail in the morning. We've so little time."

Captain Hook paced across the room and rubbed his hook and hand together, as if he were thinking.

"That's it!" he cried. "Sail! We'll shanghai Wendy and take her to sea with us. When she's gone, Peter will soon forget this mad infatuation."

Tinker Bell's eyes lit up at the thought.

"Come on, Smee," Hook called. "We must leave immediately! Surround Peter's home."

"But, Cap'n," Smee protested. "We don't know where Peter Pan lives."

Captain Hook stopped in his tracks.

"Great Scott! You're right!" he said. "What in the world will we do?"

Tinker Bell flew up in front of Hook and jingled wildly.

"What's that, my dear?" said Hook. "You could show us the way? Why, I never thought of that," he lied.

Tinker Bell dipped her foot into an inkwell, then

flew onto Hook's map of Never Land.

"X," she marked.

"Start at Pegleg Point?" Hook asked.

Tinker Bell nodded yes.

Within moments, Tinker Bell had marked out almost all the directions. She showed Hook how to go past Blindman's Bluff and across Crocodile Creek. Then Tink stopped a moment, worried. She jingled a question to the captain.

"Of course I won't harm Peter," Hook answered. "I give you my word."

Tink made her final mark on the map.

"Aha! Hangman's Tree!" Hook shouted. "So that's the entrance to his hiding place!"

With that, Hook reached over and grabbed Tinker Bell tightly in his fist. He shoved her into a lantern and latched it. He didn't need the pixie anymore. He had all the information he needed.

"Thank you, my dear," he sneered. "You've been most helpful."

Captain Hook grabbed the map and raced out the cabin door. Tinker Bell banged frantically against the lantern.

14

Across the island, the celebration at the Indian camp had come to an end. Peter and the Lost Boys danced home, whooping and chanting. At Hangman's Tree, they slipped into the secret door hidden in the tree's roots. They clambered down through the narrow caverns to their safe, underground home. There they found Wendy. She was sitting glumly, sulking.

"Big Chief Flying Eagle greets little mother," said Peter.

"Ugh!" said Wendy.

"Aw, Wendy," said Peter. "Is that all you have to say? Everyone else thinks I'm wonderful."

"Especially Tiger Lily!" said Wendy. She was still jealous of Peter and the Indian princess. "John! Michael!" Wendy yelled suddenly. "Take off that war paint and get ready for bed. You need a good night's sleep because in the morning we're going home."

"Home!" said John.

"We don't want to go home," said Michael.

Peter stepped between Wendy and the boys. He folded his arms across his chest.

"No go home!" he ordered. "Stay many moons."

"Now, Peter," said Wendy, firmly. "Let's stop pretending and be practical."

"Chief Flying Eagle has spoken!" Peter proclaimed. He stomped through the doorway and slumped down on the other side.

"Oh, for goodness' sake," Wendy said to her brothers. "Do you want to stay here and grow up like savages?"

" 'Course," said Michael.

"But you can't," Wendy explained patiently. "You need a mother. We all do."

"Aren't you our mother?" asked Michael.

"Why, Michael, of course not!" Wendy laughed. "Surely you haven't forgotten our real mother!"

She picked Michael up and hugged him on her lap.

"I'll tell you what a mother is," said Wendy. "A mother is someone who kisses your cheek. A mother is someone who whispers, 'sleep tight.' "

The other boys all gathered around. The way Wendy told it, having a mother sounded like the most wonderful thing in the world. Each of the boys found himself wishing for a mother of his own.

"I propose we leave for home at once!" said John.

"Could I come, too, Wendy?" asked Cubby.

"Me, too, Wendy!" cried all the Lost Boys.

"All right, boys," Wendy smiled. "I'm sure Mother would be glad to have you. That is, if Peter doesn't mind."

"Go on!" Peter called from the doorway. He'd been listening all the while. "Go back and grow up! But I'm warning you. Once you're grown up, you can never come back. Never!"

Peter was not the only one who'd been listening to Wendy. Up above ground, Captain Hook and Mr. Smee bent over the tree roots. Behind them were the pirates, armed and lying in wait.

"Well, men," said John. "Shall we be off?"

"Yeah!" cried the Lost Boys. "Come on! Let's go!"

They scrambled up to the secret door. Peter picked up his pipes and started to play.

"Good-bye, Peter," said Wendy.

Peter didn't answer, so Wendy followed the boys. When she got outside, she gasped at what she saw. Pirates! All the boys were bound and gagged. One of the pirates grabbed Wendy.

"Away with them, men!" shouted Captain Hook.

Wendy and the boys kicked and screamed as

the pirates carried them away. Captain Hook laughed. In his hands he held a small, brightly wrapped box.

"And now, Smee, to take care of Master Peter Pan," he said.

He tied a rope around the box and lowered it into Peter Pan's hideout.

15

When the pirates reached the boat, they tied Wendy and the boys to the mast. Captain Hook surveyed his prisoners. The boys would be his new recruits. Surely they'd jump at the chance to lead a pirate's life, a life full of adventure. Captain Hook paced before the mast.

"I'll tell you what I'll do," he said to the boys. "All those who sign up without delay will get a free tattoo. And I'll be frank," he added, "if you don't join, you walk the plank. The choice is yours."

One of the pirates cut the rope that bound Wendy and the boys. The boys raced to sign up with Hook. Wendy clapped her hands angrily.

"Boys!" she shouted. The boys stopped in their tracks. "Aren't you ashamed of yourselves!"

"But we'll have to walk the plank if we don't," said Cubby.

"Oh, no, we won't," said Wendy. "Peter Pan will save us."

Hook poked Smee and the two burst out laughing.

"Peter Pan will save them," Hook laughed.

Hook and Smee laughed harder. Wendy stared at them, puzzled. Across the deck, Tinker Bell watched them, too. She was still caged in the lantern, and she no longer trusted Hook at all.

"A thousand pardons," Hook said to Wendy. "I don't believe you are in on our little joke. You see, we left a present for Peter," he said, "a sort of surprise package, you might say. Why, I can see our little friend at this very moment, reading the tender inscription. 'To Peter. With love from Wendy.' "

Wendy started. What was Hook talking about? She'd written no such note.

"The tag says, 'Do not open until six o'clock,' " Hook continued. "And in that package is an ingenious little device that will blast Peter Pan out of Never Land forever . . . just as the clock strikes six."

Six o'clock! The hour was but eighteen seconds away! Tinker Bell knocked over the lantern and escaped.

In his underground hideout, Peter was examining the package. He had already begun to untie it when Tinker Bell flew in and tried to grab it out of his hands.

"Hey, stop!" shouted Peter. "This is a package

from Wendy. What's the matter with you?"

Tink jingled excitedly.

"Hook?" Peter said. "A bomb? Don't be ridiculous."

Peter looked down at the package in his lap. It had started to smoke. Tink dove at the box to push it away from Peter. The box exploded in a blinding flash. The room clouded up with its thick, black smoke.

Back at the ship, Wendy, the boys, and the pirates all heard the terrible explosion. Hook took off his hat and held it mockingly over his heart.

"And so passeth a worthy opponent," he said.

"Amen," chuckled Smee.

16

When the smoke cleared, Peter was still alive. He crawled out from the debris and called for Tink. He heard a faint jingling sound.

"Tink, where are you?" he called.

Peter spotted Tinker Bell's light flickering under an avalanche of rubble.

"Tink, are you all right?" he asked.

Tink jingled something.

"Wendy? The boys?" Peter said. "But I gotta save *you* first."

Peter crawled toward Tink's light. The light began to fade.

"Hold on!" Peter called. "Don't go out!"

While Peter worked to save Tink, Captain Hook gave Wendy and the boys one last chance. They could sign up with him or they could walk the plank.

"Which will it be?" he said.

"We'll never join your crew," Wendy said proudly.

"As you wish," smiled Captain Hook. He pointed to the plank. "Ladies first, my dear."

The pirates shoved Wendy onto the plank. Wendy took a deep breath. This was it. She walked slowly, steadily to the edge. She looked down. There was nothing left to do. She jumped. Hook, Smee, and the pirates waited for the splash. There was none.

"Cap'n!" said Smee. "Not a sound!"

Far below, just above the water, Wendy clung to Peter. He had flown to her rescue just in time. Tinker Bell was with them. The three flew up to the crow's nest.

"Who's next?" Hook challenged angrily.

"You're next, Hook!" Peter shouted down. "This time you've gone too far!"

"It's Pan!" shouted the boys.

"It can't be!" gasped Hook.

Captain Hook drew his sword. Peter drew his knife. Hook lunged at Peter. Peter flew out of reach.

"Come on, everybody!" Peter called to the boys.

The boys climbed up the rigging to the safety of the crow's nest.

"Get those scurvy brats!" shouted Hook.

In the water below, the crocodile swam up to the ship. If there was a duel, Hook might lose. The crocodile licked his chops. He was waiting for dinner.

17

Peter flew at Hook and backed him up onto the plank. He slashed at Hook's hat and cut off the plume.

This is no mere boy!" Hook gasped. " 'Tis a flying devil!"

Mr. Smee ran for the rowboat and dropped it into the water. The other pirates climbed the rigging to get to the crow's nest. They carried their knives clamped in their teeth. The children in the crow's nest aimed their weapons.

"Fire!" John shouted the order.

The children threw whatever was at hand at the bloodthirsty pirates. The pirates braced themselves against the attack and then kept climbing.

Tink flew frantically to Peter's ear and jingled for help. Peter had to do something to save his friends, but first he had to fend off Hook. He flew at Hook feet first and knocked the captain back. Then he flew up at the pirates climbing toward the crow's nest. He slashed at the rigging with

his knife. The ropes gave way and the pirates fell screaming into the rowboat below.

Hook jumped up and shook his fist at Peter.

"Fly! Fly, you coward!" he screamed.

"Coward? Me?" Peter stopped.

"You wouldn't dare fight old Hook man to man," Hook yelled. "You fly away like a cowardly sparrow."

"Nobody calls Pan a coward!" Peter cried. "I'll fight you man-to-man!"

"You mean you won't fly?" Hook sneered.

"No, Peter!" shouted Wendy. "Don't agree to it! It's a trick!"

Peter stared the pirate in the eye. "I give you my word, Hook," he said.

Hook and Peter drew their weapons. They climbed up to the yardarm, dueling with each step. Hook knocked Peter down and stomped on his hand. He kicked Peter's knife out of the boy's grasp. Peter scrambled for his weapon, but Hook grabbed it up.

"Now!" Hook cried. He poked his sword threateningly at Peter's chest, ready to pierce the boy's heart. "Insolent youth!" he said. "Prepare to die!"

"Fly, Peter!" cried Wendy. "Fly, Peter! Fly!"

18

Peter looked up at the gleaming sword.

"No!" he said resolutely. "I gave my word!"

His eyes darted quickly, searching for anything he might use to defend himself. Behind Captain Hook flew a large, silken pirate flag. Peter jumped out from under the tip of the sword and pulled the flapping flag down. It fell over Hook. Hook stumbled blindly. Peter grabbed his sword and knocked the pirate down.

"You're mine, Hook!" Peter shouted.

Up in the crow's nest, the children all cheered.

"Off with his head!" they shouted.

"Cleave him to the brisket!" yelled Michael.

Hook trembled under the point of his own sword.

"You wouldn't do old Hook in, now would you, lad?" he pleaded. "I'll do anything you say."

"Well, all right," Peter agreed. "If you say you're a codfish."

"I'm a codfish!" shouted Hook.

"Louder!" said Peter. He poked Hook again with the sword.

"I'm a codfish!" Hook shouted louder.

"Hooray!" the children all cheered. "Hook is a codfish! Hook is a codfish!"

"All right, Hook," said Peter. "You're free to go. And never return!" Peter lifted the sword and threw it aside.

Hook stood up. He smiled a sly smile. When Peter turned his back, Hook snuck up behind him.

"Peter!" shouted Wendy.

Hook swung at Peter with his sharp, hooked hand. As Peter flew to safety, Hook fell backwards. He lost his balance and fell off the yardarm.

"AHHHHHHHH!"

The crocodile was in the water below, waiting for the captain. The crocodile opened his jaws wide. Hook fell right in.

The crocodile snapped his mouth shut, but Hook struggled to get free. He pried the crocodile's mouth open and tried frantically to swim away.

"Smee!" Hook cried.

Smee and the pirates were in the rowboat. The captain tried to swim to them. The crocodile slipped quickly through the water. He was right at Hook's toes. Hook thrashed and paddled faster out to sea. The crocodile stayed right on his tail.

"Cap'n!" called Smee. "Wait for us!"

On the deck of the ship, the children all cheered.

Peter put on Hook's hat and picked up his sword.

"Hooray for Captain Pan!" the children cried.

"All right, ya swabs," said Peter. "Aloft with ya! We're casting off. Heave those halyards!"

Wendy curtsied to the ship's new captain.

"Captain Pan," she said. "Could you please tell me, sir, where we're sailing?"

"To London, Madam," Peter said.

"Oh, Peter!" Wendy cried. "Michael! John! We're going home!"

The Lost Boys hoisted the anchor. Tinker Bell flew over the ship, sprinkling pixie dust across it. The ship lifted up out of the water. It flew up into the clouds and over the island. Wendy and her brothers were leaving Never Land.

19

In the dark London night, Big Ben chimed the late hour. Mr. and Mrs. Darling had come home from their party. Mr. Darling unhooked Nana from her chain and the three climbed the stairs to the nursery.

"Oh, George," said Mrs. Darling. "I'm so glad you changed your mind about Wendy. After all, she's still just a child."

"Oh, pshaw, Mary," Mr. Darling chuckled. "You know I never mean those things. Do I, Nana?" he patted the old dog on the head.

Mrs. Darling opened the nursery door and glanced at Wendy's bed. It was empty!

Nana ran to the window seat. There was Wendy, asleep on the cushion, in front of an open window.

"Wendy!" Mrs. Darling cried. "What on earth are you doing there?"

Wendy opened her eyes and blinked at the figures around her.

"Oh, Mother!" she said. "We're back!"

"Back?" asked Mr. Darling.

"All except the Lost Boys," Wendy said. "They weren't quite ready."

"Lost Boys?" asked Mr. Darling. "Ready?"

"To grow up," Wendy explained. "That's why they went back to Never Land."

Her father shook his head, confused. "Never Land?"

"But I'm ready," Wendy sighed. "Ready to grow up."

"Well, my dear," her father ruffled her hair. "All in good time."

Wendy ran to her mother and threw her arms around her waist.

"Oh, but, Mother," she said. "It was such a wonderful adventure. Tinker Bell and the mermaids and Peter Pan . . . he was the most wonderful of all!"

Her mother tucked the bed covers around John and Michael.

"Why, even when we were kidnapped . . ." Wendy chattered on.

"Kidnapped!" shouted her father.

". . . I knew Peter Pan would save us!" Wendy said. "And he did! And we all called him a codfish. Captain Hook, I mean. And then we sailed away on a ship in the sky."

Mr. Darling yawned at the fantastic story.

Wendy ran back to the windowseat and stared out at the night.

"Oh, Mother, he really is wonderful, isn't he?" she cried. "See how well he sails the ship."

Mrs. Darling followed her daughter's gaze.

"George!" she cried.

High in the sky, sailing past the clouds, was a sparkling, glitter-dusted ship.

Mr. Darling gasped.

Wendy and her father and mother stood at the window, staring out through the dark.

"You know," said Mr. Darling. "I have the strangest feeling that I've seen that ship before. A long time ago. When I was very young."

Mrs. Darling smiled knowingly and put her arm around her husband.

The ship passed in front of the full, bright moon. In the days to come, as Wendy said, she would indeed grow up. But Wendy would always remember Peter Pan and the magical time she had had in Never Land.